≷ Campsite Creature ≷

MOLLY MAC

by MARTY KELLEY

First published in 2019 by Raintree, an imprint of Capstone
Global Library Limited, 264 Banbury Road, Oxford, OX2 7DY -
Registered company number: 6695582

www.raintree.co.uk

Text © 2018 Marty Kelley
Illustrations © 2018 Marty Kelley

The author's moral rights are hereby asserted.

All characters in this publication are fictitious and any
resemblance to real persons, living or dead, is purely coincidental.

ISBN 978 1 4747 6720 0

22 21 20 19 18

10 9 8 7 6 5 4 3 2 1

A CIP catalogue for this book is available from the British Library.

Education Consultant: Julie Lemire
Editor: Shelly Lyons
Designer: Ashlee Suker

Printed and bound in India

Contents

All About Me!

A picture of me!

Name:
Molly Mac

People in my family:
Mum
Dad
Drooly baby brother Alex

My best friend: KAYLEY!!!!

I really like:
Crunchy delicious tacos!
But not if they have tomatoes on them.
Yuck! They are squirty and wet.

When I grow up I want to be:
An artist. And a famous animal trainer.
And a professional taco taster. And a teacher.
And a superhero. And a dinner lady. And a pirate!

My special memory: Kayley and I camped in my
garden. We toasted marshmallows with cheese.
They were surprisingly un-delicious.

Chapter 1

No toaster, no tacos

Krrrshhhh. Krrrshhhh.

Molly Mac slid the toaster oven across the worktop towards her backpack.

"Molly Mac?" asked Mum.

"Don't ask," said Molly.

"I'm asking," said Mum. "What are you doing with the toaster oven?"

"I'm packing it for our camping trip," Molly said. "Tonight is Taco Night. I need the toaster to warm the taco shells."

"Well, Molly—"

"I will also need the fridge, so the cheese stays fresh!" said Molly.

Mum slid the toaster back where it belonged. "We're going camping, Molly," she said. "No toaster. No tacos. We are going to cook dinner over a campfire tonight!"

Dad walked into the kitchen and picked up a cool box. "And we'll be toasting marshmallows!" he sang as he opened the kitchen door to go outside. "Marshmallows are my favourite vegetable. I'm going to eat about a million of them!"

Molly sighed. "I was hoping to eat about a million tacos tonight," she replied.

"Did somebody say tacos?" Grandpa Kevin asked. He walked into the kitchen holding Molly's baby brother, Alex. "Maybe Alex and I will eat tacos all weekend while you are all off in the woods."

Alex gurgled and laughed.

Molly patted Grandpa Kevin on the shoulder. "Sorry, buddy," she said. "Neither of you has enough teeth to eat crunchy tacos."

Grandpa Kevin laughed. "Do you know what I have got, though?" he said.

"An emergency taco kit that I can take camping?" Molly asked.

"Even better," Grandpa Kevin told her. He handed Molly a small, wrapped present. "This is from Gram and me."

Molly unwrapped the present. It was a shiny red camera.

"We got it so you could take some fun pictures of your camping trip this weekend," Grandpa Kevin explained. "You can show us the pictures when you get back."

"Wow!" Molly cried. "Thanks!" She gave Grandpa Kevin a big hug and held up the camera. **"Say cheese!"**

Click!

"That's exciting," Mum said. "Did you know that our newspaper has a photo contest every week? You could send in one of your photos. They might put it in the paper."

"Really?" Molly asked. "I could be a real, live, professional photo-taker! Let's get going! I have some exciting photos to take!"

"We will leave as soon as Kayley gets here," Mum said. "Are you all packed?"

Molly nodded. "Almost," she said as she picked up her backpack. "I just need one more thing. Where do we keep the hippo spray?"

"Hippo spray?" Mum asked.

"Don't ask," Molly said as she ran up to her room.

Chapter 2

Wild hippos!

Molly and Kayley sat in the back of the car.

"This is going to be so much fun," Kayley said. "Thanks for inviting me to come camping with you."

"I'm glad you could come," Molly told her. "Everything is more fun with you." She held up her camera. "Say **Tacos!**"

Kayley laughed. **"Tacos!"**

Click!

"I'm going to be a real, live, professional photo-taker," Molly said. "And my amazing photo is going to be in a real, live newspaper!"

"Wow!" Kayley said. "What are you going to take a photo of?"

Molly leaned over towards Kayley. "That's the most exciting part!" she whispered. "Seeing as we'll be out in the woods, I'm going to take a photo of a wild hippo!"

Kayley's eyes grew wide. "A wild hippo?" she gasped.

Molly nodded. "There is one problem, though. I couldn't find any hippo spray. It's like insect spray. Except it keeps hippos from squishing you when you take their photo."

Kayley shook her head. "I don't think there are any hippos in the woods around here, Molly," she said.

"Are you sure?" Molly asked. "I read that they live near rivers in Africa. There is a river at the campsite, and we have to drive for almost two hours to get there. After driving for that long, we'll probably be in Africa."

"I don't think so," Kayley told her.

Molly's shoulders slumped. "How can I be a professional photo-taker if there are no wild hippos to take photos of?"

Kayley smiled and opened her bag. She pulled out her toy dog. **"I brought Herman!"** she said as she laughed.

Molly held up her camera. "Look wild, Herman," she said.

Click!

"I don't think Herman is wild enough," Molly sighed.

Kayley took a book out of her bag. "How about this?" she asked. She held it up so Molly could see the title – *Bear and Rabbit Go Camping*.

"A book?" Molly groaned. "A book is even less wild than Herman. A book is the exact opposite of wild."

Kayley opened the book and pointed to a picture. It showed a bear and rabbit toasting marshmallows over a campfire. The rabbit was saying, "I love toasted marshmallows." The bear was saying, "Me, too!"

"Rabbits like toasted marshmallows," Kayley said to Molly. "It says so right here in the book. We have marshmallows. Maybe a rabbit will come to our campsite. Then you can take its photo!"

Molly looked at the picture. "The book says that bears like toasted marshmallows, too! Bears are **WAY** more exciting than rabbits. I'm going to take a photo of a bear!"

Kayley shook her head. "That's not a good idea, Molly."

"I know," Molly said. "It's a **GREAT** idea."

Bigfoot

Crack! Snap! Crrrrrack!

At the campsite, Dad made a roaring fire in the fire pit. Mum helped Molly and Kayley put hot dogs on sticks so they could cook them over the fire.

"Are you sure we can't toast tacos over the campfire?" Molly asked.

"Positive," Mum said. "We can have tacos anytime."

"Like right now?" Molly asked.

Mum sighed. "No, Molly. **No tacos.** Cook your hot dog."

Kayley held up her stick. "Mine has two points!" she said. "I can cook two hot dogs at once!"

Dad held up a stick with lots of small branches on the end. "Well, I can cook a million hot dogs at once!" he said as he

laughed. "And then, when we're ready to toast marshmallows, I can cook a million of them, too!"

"Speaking of marshmallows," Molly said, "could I possibly have a few marshmallows for later?"

"I'm pretty sure that there won't be any marshmallows left after Dad starts eating them," Mum said. "He's totally **koo-koo** about marshmallows. And do I even want to know why you want marshmallows for later?"

"Probably not," Molly said. "I want to take an exciting photo, but there are no hippos in the area. Herman isn't wild enough, but Kayley's book says that rabbits love toasted marshmallows. But they're not as exciting as bears who also love marshmallows."

"Bears?" Mum said.

"Bears?" Dad said.

"Bears," Molly said. "They really **LOVE** marshmallows. It was in a book, so it must be true. I'm going to stick some marshmallows in my sleeping bag. When a bear comes to eat them, I can take its photo."

"Molly–" said Mum.

"I'll have an exciting photo so I can be a professional photo-taker," Molly said. "Then I'll feed marshmallows to the bear so it won't eat me."

"Molly, honey," Dad said. "There are no bears around here. And even if there were, you shouldn't feed animals. Marshmallows are not good for them." He popped a marshmallow in his mouth. "But they're great for me. And do you know who else likes marshmallows?"

"Who?" Molly asked.

Dad got a bit closer to the fire. "Bigfoot," he whispered.

"Bigfoot?" gasped Molly and Kayley.

Dad nodded. "Bigfoot. He's a big, hairy creature who lives in the woods."

"A big, hairy creature?" cried Molly. "Like Uncle Dave?"

"Not like Uncle Dave," Dad said. "Bigfoot is even bigger and hairier than Uncle Dave."

"Whoa!" Molly gasped. "I didn't think that was possible."

Dad pointed to the dark woods around the campsite. Orange light from the fire danced in the tree branches. "Nobody knows what he really is or what he looks like," he said.

"Why not?" Molly asked. "Can't they just look him up on the internet?"

"They could," Dad said, "but nobody has ever taken a good photo of him. Some people say he's not real. But other people think he could be anywhere. Even right here! **GRRRRRR!**" Dad growled and held his torch under his chin. **"GRRRRRRRR! GIVE ME YOUR MARSHMALLOWS!!"**

Molly and Kayley both screamed.

"All right," Mum said. "I think that's enough scary campfire stories. Who wants some marshmallows?"

After eating lots of gooey, toasted marshmallows, Molly and Kayley climbed into their sleeping bags.

"I'm glad there are no bears around here," Kayley said. "But now what are you going to take a photo of?"

Molly smiled and held up her camera. "Oh, I'm going to get a photo of something way better than a bear."

"Herman?" laughed Kayley. She held Herman up to the camera.

Click!

"Even better than Herman," Molly said. "I'm going to get a photo of **Bigfoot.**"

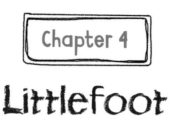

Littlefoot

Ziiiiiiiiiiiip.

The next morning, Molly slipped out of her sleeping bag. She grabbed her camera and opened the tent. She poked her head out.

"Wow!" she said.

She shook Kayley awake. "Kayley! Kayley! You have to see this! Wake up! Wake up!"

Kayley rubbed her eyes and yawned. "What is it?" she asked.

Molly pointed to the tent flap. **"Come and see! Come and see!"**

Kayley groaned and rolled over.

Molly shook her shoulder. "Come on!"

Kayley wiggled out of her sleeping bag and crawled over to the opening. She poked her head out. "What?" she asked. "I can't see anything."

Molly slipped past Kayley and hopped out of the tent. She pointed to the ground. **"Look!"** she cried. **"Bigfoot was here!"**

"Bigfoot?" Kayley asked. She climbed out of the tent and looked where Molly was pointing. There were a lot of small footprints in the soft ground.

"Those footprints don't look very big to me," Kayley said.

Molly pointed to the picnic table. "And look what Bigfoot did!"

The bag of marshmallows was torn apart. Small pieces of it were scattered on the table.

Molly took a photo of the shredded plastic.

Click!

She took a photo of the footprints on the ground.

Click!

"I can't believe I didn't get a photo of Bigfoot," Molly groaned. "How did we sleep through a Bigfoot attack? He must have been here for hours. He ate ALL the marshmallows!"

Kayley shook her head. "These footprints are really small, Molly," she said. "I don't think this was Bigfoot."

Ziiiiiiiiip!

Mum unzipped her tent flap and climbed out of the tent.

"Good morning, girls," she said. "What are you doing up so early?"

"Ahhh!" Molly cried. **"It's not Bigfoot. It's Bedhead!"**

She took Mum's photo.

Click!

"Very funny," Mum grumbled. "What are you doing out here?"

Molly pointed to the ground. "Bigfoot was here!" She pointed to the mess on the picnic table. "He ate the rest of our marshmallows!"

Mum looked at the footprints on the ground. "Molly," she said. "Those are not Bigfoot tracks. There is no such thing as Bigfoot. Dad was just telling you a spooky campfire story last night."

"No such thing as Bigfoot? Then what made these footprints?" Molly asked. "And what ate our marshmallows? Do you think it was a hippo? I **KNEW** I should have brought hippo spray!"

Mum shrugged. "They look like raccoon footprints," she said. "Dad must have forgotten to pack away the marshmallows before we went to bed. I'm going to get a jumper. Then we can tidy up and have some breakfast."

Mum climbed back into her tent.

"I'm glad it wasn't Bigfoot," Kayley said. "He sounded a bit scary. Now maybe you can take a photo of a raccoon!"

"It wasn't Bigfoot," Molly said. "And it wasn't a hippo. And I don't think this was a raccoon, either."

"Then what do you think made these footprints?" Kayley asked. "Your mum said it was a raccoon."

"I think Mum just said that so we wouldn't be scared," Molly said. She held up her camera.

"Maybe," said Kayley.

"But I'm not scared," Molly continued. "I'm excited. I didn't get a photo of Bigfoot, but now I'm going to get a photo of something even more exciting. I'm going to get a photo of . . . **Littlefoot!**"

Chapter 5

Bathroom Bigfoot

After breakfast, Molly and Kayley walked along the road through the campsite.

Kayley pointed at a small butterfly on a flower. "You could take a photo of a butterfly!"

Molly sighed. "A butterfly isn't an exciting, wild animal. We need to find **Littlefoot.** We don't have much time. Mum and Dad said we could walk around this loop while they drink coffee."

"Then we're going swimming in the river!" Kayley said. "I can't wait!"

"I'm still hoping that we might see a hippo in the river," Molly said.

"I don't think so, Molly," Kayley said. She pointed to a branch in a tree. "There is a bird over in that tree. You could take a photo of a bird."

Molly sighed again. "This campsite has some pretty disappointing wild animals," said Molly. "We really need to find **Littlefoot.**"

Molly kicked a pine cone. It tumbled along the road and settled in some leaves. She ran over to it to kick it again. **"Look!"** she cried.

Kayley ran over to look.

Molly pointed at the ground. "More of Littlefoot's tracks!" she whispered. "Let's follow them! Maybe they will lead us to his top-secret underground lair."

Molly trotted along the side of the road, following the trail of small footprints. Kayley crept along beside her. "What are we going to do if we find Littlefoot's top-secret underground lair?" Kayley asked.

"We will sneak in and take his photo!" Molly said.

"I don't think this is a good idea, Molly," Kayley said. "What if Littlefoot **EATS** us?"

"He's not going to eat us," Molly said. "He only eats marshmallows. And tacos. Because everybody loves tacos. Even mysterious wild creatures who live in . . . **WAIT!**"

Molly skidded to a stop.

Kayley bumped into her.

"What is it?" Kayley whispered. "Is it **Littlefoot?**"

Molly pointed to some strange tracks. The tracks crossed the road and went along a small path through the bushes. They looked like huge footprints.

"It's definitely not Littlefoot," Molly said. "It must be **Bigfoot!** Dad wasn't making him up! Come on!"

Molly held up her camera and tip-toed along the short path. Kayley crept along behind her.

Through the bushes, they could see a small building. The footprints led right up to a door on the side of the building.

"It's Bigfoot's house!" Molly whispered.

"I don't think so," Kayley said. She pointed to a sign on the side of the building that said "Showers & Toilets."

"Do you think Bigfoot is taking a shower?" Kayley asked.

"Maybe," Molly said. "Or he might be–"

SCREEEECH!

The door of the building was pushed open by a big, hairy arm.

"It's Bigfoot!" cried Kayley. **"HIDE!"**

Kayley and Molly hopped into the bushes at the side of the path.

Molly held up her camera and took a photo just as the hairy creature stepped out of the building.

CLICK!

It started walking right towards them. It was wearing purple flip-flops and was holding a small basket full of shampoo, soap and toothpaste.

It wasn't Bigfoot.

It was a hairy, smiling man.

"Good morning, ladies!" he said to Molly and Kayley as he passed by their hiding place in the bushes.

He whistled a happy tune as he walked away down the path.

"That wasn't Bigfoot," Molly sighed.

"He was pretty hairy, though," Kayley said.

"Even hairier than Uncle Dave," Molly agreed. "But I still need to take an exciting photo."

"I know!" Kayley said. "You can take a photo of me doing a cannonball into the river! Let's go swimming!"

Chapter 6

Midnight marshmallow madness

Crackle, crackle, POP!

That night, they all sat around the campfire. Sparks danced through the air when Dad added another log to the roaring fire.

"I have a big surprise for tonight!" Dad sang.

"We're cooking tacos on sticks?" Molly asked.

"This is even better than tacos," Dad said.

"Excuse me, Dad," Molly said. She patted Dad's arm. "I think we can all agree that nothing is better than tacos."

"Oh, this is," Dad said. He reached into a bag next to his chair.

"Did you get hippo spray?" asked Molly.

Dad shook his head. "I bought some more marshmallows at the campsite shop this afternoon while you were swimming with Mum."

"Hmmm . . . ," Molly said. "Marshmallows are just what I need tonight."

"Me, too," Dad said. "Marshmallows are just what I need every night!"

He popped one in his mouth.

"You ate it **raw?**" Molly gasped. "Can you do that?"

"I can," Dad said. "But *you* have to eat dinner first."

After dinner, everyone toasted marshmallows.

"Watch this!" Dad said.

He stuffed one marshmallow after another on his stick. Just as he was squeezing the tenth marshmallow on, the stick broke.

SNAP!

"Darn!" Dad said. "Now I need a new stick."

Mum switched on her torch. "I'll help you look," she said.

"Try to find a nice, strong one that can hold **FIFTY** marshmallows at once," Dad said.

"I'll try," laughed Mum.

They got up and looked around the campsite for a new stick for Dad.

Molly put her stick down and sneaked over to the bag of marshmallows. She grabbed a handful of them.

"What are you doing with all those marshmallows, Molly?" asked Kayley.

Molly held a hand up to her lips. "Shhhhhh!" she whispered. "Don't ask."

"I'm asking," Kayley said.

Molly stuffed the marshmallows in her pocket. "Tonight, I'm going to sneak out of the tent and put these marshmallows on the ground. Then, when Littlefoot comes to eat them, I can take his photo!"

Molly sat back down just as Mum and Dad came back with a new stick.

"Oh, boy!" said Dad. **"Look at this beauty!"**

He held up a stick with four points on the end. "Can somebody pass me four marshmallows, please?"

When they had finished toasting marshmallows, Dad packed up the food. He put the marshmallows safely in the cool box and latched it shut.

"We don't want any more midnight visitors," he said.

"Oh, yes we do," Molly chuckled.

Chapter 7

Midnight visitor

Schhlllp. Schhhlllp. Schloop.

"Molly, what are you doing?" Kayley whispered.

"I'm trying to get these marshmallows out of my pocket," Molly whispered back. "I think they melted when I sat next to the fire."

She pulled her hand out of her pocket and licked the gooey mess off her fingers.

"I suppose you won't be able to put them outside for Littlefoot," Kayley said.

"Maybe I can just lay my hand outside and wait for Littlefoot to come and lick it," Molly said. She wiggled her sticky fingers in the air.

"Ewwww," groaned Kayley. "I don't think you should–"

"Shhhh!" Molly hissed. "Did you hear that?"

There was a small shuffling sound outside the tent.

Kayley's eyes grew wide. **"What is that?"** she whispered.

Molly picked up her camera. "It must be Littlefoot!" she whispered.

The shuffling sounds outside the tent stopped. There was a quiet squeak.

"He's opening the cool box to get the rest of the marshmallows!" Molly whispered.

Molly unzipped the tent flap and hopped out of the tent.

Something big was standing in front of the cool box stuffing marshmallows in its mouth.

"AH HA!" she cried. **"It's not Littlefoot. It's BIGFOOT!"**

She held up her camera.

Click!

The next day after breakfast, Molly and Kayley helped Mum and Dad pack up the campsite.

"Ohhhhh," Dad groaned. "I have such a stomach ache."

"I'm not surprised," Mum said. "You ate almost the whole bag of marshmallows on your little midnight adventure last night."

"And I didn't get a photo of Littlefoot," Molly grumbled. "All I got was a picture of Dad with a face full of marshmallows. Maybe we can come back to the campsite next weekend so I can have another try."

Dad groaned again. "I don't think we'll be camping for a while," he said.

"Maybe next weekend, we can go on a trip to the beach," Mum suggested.

"The beach?" Molly asked.
She held up her camera and
smiled. "Do we have any
sea-monster spray?" she asked.

"Do I even want to know why
you think you need sea-monster
spray?" Mum asked.

"Probably not," Molly said.

All About Me!

A picture of me!

Name:
Marty Kelley

People in my family:
My lovely wife, Kerri
My amazing son, Alex
My terrific daughter, Tori

I really like: Pizza! And hiking in the woods. And being with my friends. And reading. And making music. And traveling with my family.

When I grow up I want to be:
A rock star drummer!

My special memory:
Sitting on the couch with my kids and reading a huge pile of books together.

Find more at my website: www.martykelley.com

MORE
MOLLY MAC

Meet Molly Mac, the curious girl who is always up to something. She's a whirlwind full of questions, and she's out to find the answers!

LUCKY'S STEAKHOUSE

Lucky Break
by MARTY KELLEY

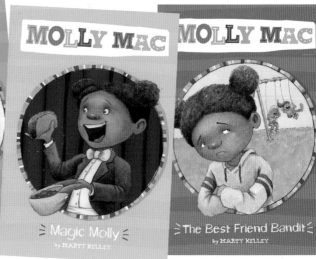

Magic Molly
by MARTY KELLEY

The Best Friend Bandit
by MARTY KELLEY

Sammy's Great Escape
by MARTY KELLEY

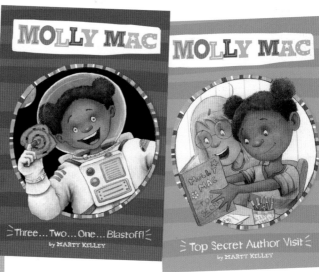

Three... Two... One... Blastoff!
by MARTY KELLEY

Top Secret Author Visit
by MARTY KELLEY